KU-636-986

CONTENTS

MEET THE MYSTERY INC. GANG!

SHAGGY

Norville "Shaggy" Rogers is a laid-back dude who would rather search for food than clues . . . but he usually finds both!

SCOOBY-DOO

A happy hound with a super snout, Scooby-Doo is the mascot of Mystery Inc. He'll do anything for a Scooby Snack!

FRED

Fred Jones, Jr. is the oldest member of the group. Friendly and fun-loving, he's a good sport – and good at them too.

SCOOBY-DOO!
MINI MYSTERIES

REDBEARD'S REVENGE

by John Sazaklis   Illustrated by Christian Cornia

WALTHAM FOREST LIBRARIES

904 000 00731964

Raintree is an imprint of Capstone Global Library Limited, a company incorporated in England and Wales having its registered office at 264 Banbury Road, Oxford, OX2 7DY – Registered company number: 6695582

www.raintree.co.uk
myorders@raintree.co.uk

Copyright © 2022 Hanna-Barbera.
SCOOBY-DOO and all related characters
and elements © & ™ Hanna-Barbera. (s22)
The moral rights of the proprietor have been asserted.

All rights reserved. No part of this publication may be reproduced in any form or by any means (including photocopying or storing it in any medium by electronic means and whether or not transiently or incidentally to some other use of this publication) without the written permission of the copyright owner, except in accordance with the provisions of the Copyright, Designs and Patents Act 1988 or under the terms of a licence issued by the Copyright Licensing Agency, 5th Floor, Shackleton House, 4 Battle Bridge Lane, London SE1 2HX (www. cla.co.uk). Applications for the copyright owner's written permission should be addressed to the publisher.

Designed by Tracy Davies
Original illustrations © Capstone Global Library Limited 2022
Originated by Capstone Global Library Ltd
Printed and bound in India

978 1 3982 2596 1

British Library Cataloguing in Publication Data
A full catalogue record for this book is available from the British Library.

Desi

WALTHAM FOREST LIBRARIES	
904 000 00731964	
Askews & Holts	06-Jul-2022
JF NEW	⊢

DAPHNE

Brainy and bold, the fashion-forward Daphne Blake solves mysteries with street smarts and a sense of style.

VELMA

Velma Dinkley is clever and book smart. She may be the youngest member of the team, but she's an old pro at cracking cases.

MYSTERY MACHINE

Not only is this van the gang's main way of getting around, but it is stocked with all the equipment needed for every adventure.

CHAPTER ONE

REDBEARD APPEARS

The Mystery Inc. gang pulled up to a huge mansion and piled out of the Mystery Machine. They had been called by Mr Magnus, the shipping tycoon, to crack a case.

A butler opened the huge door. They followed him into Magnus Manor.

Mr and Mrs Magnus were in a state of shock.

"The cargo has been stolen from all his ships," Mrs Magnus said.

"It was Redbeard!" Mr Magnus yelled. "I saw him with my own eyes!"

"Redbeard?" Velma asked. "The legendary pirate from hundreds of years ago?"

"That would mean you saw a ghost," Fred said.

"Like, did he say g-ghost?" Shaggy asked Scooby-Doo.

The gang went to the dock to investigate. A worker pointed out the ship that belonged to Mr Magnus.

"We've got a job to do," Daphne said. "Let's go!"

Just then, a mysterious fog rolled in. It covered the dock and made the ship hard to see.

All of a sudden, the ship began to glow with an eerie light!

The Mystery Inc. gang climbed aboard the empty ship. **THUMP! THUMP! THUMP!** They heard the sound of a wooden leg.

Suddenly, a scary-looking pirate appeared.

"ARGH!"

CHAPTER TWO

THE PESKY PIRATE

"ZOINKS!" Shaggy shouted. "Like, it's Redbeard!"

"And re's really real!" Scooby-Doo said, panicked.

The members of Mystery Inc. ran away as fast as they could.

The ghost ship was full of twists
and turns.

"Jeepers!" Daphne said. "I found a
room full of costumes!"

"And weapons," added Fred.

The gang dressed and grabbed some weapons.

"We are ready for that red-headed robber," Velma said.

"Like, now we can catch Redbeard red-handed!" Shaggy added.

"I have a groovy idea, gang," Fred said. "Let's split up and search the spooky ship."

Daphne and Velma went one way. Scooby and Shaggy went another. Fred was left all alone.

"Hmm," Fred said to himself. "Guess it wasn't such a groovy idea."

Suddenly, Redbeard appeared and grabbed Fred.

"**AHOY, MATEY!**" cried the crook. "You're mine!"

Shaggy and Scooby-Doo heard a strange noise.

CLANK! CLANK! CLANK!

They climbed to the deck and saw Fred walking the plank!

"RUH-ROH!" screamed Scooby.

The pesky pirate appeared behind the duo.

"ZOINKS!" shouted Shaggy.

"Quit blubberin' ye landlubbers!" growled the ghost.

CHAPTER THREE

BUBBLE TROUBLE

Redbeard took the frightened friends to the galley. The creepy crook made them cook for him.

Scooby-Doo poured lots and lots of lemon juice into the pot. But it was really lemon-scented soap!

The room filled with big, soapy

bubbles. Redbeard was trapped!

Daphne and Velma found their

friends and aimed their weapons.

POP! CRASH!

Redbeard landed hard on the floor. His mask popped off.

"It's Mr Magnus!" Shaggy shouted.

"JINKIES!" Velma said. "There was no greedy ghost!"

"Mr Magnus kept the cargo instead of giving it to the owners," added Daphne.

"And I would have got away with it," yelled Mr Magnus, "if not for you meddling kids!"

An officer arrived to take the terrible tycoon away.

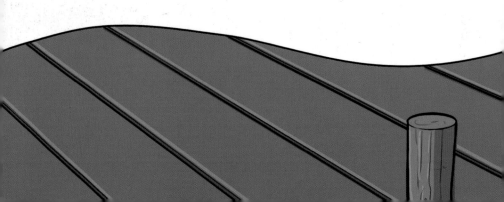

"Another mystery solved by Mystery Inc.," Fred said.

"A job well done," Velma agreed.

"That's right!" Daphne said.

"Like, I think it's time we set sail for home," Shaggy said.

Scooby agreed.

"SCOOBY-DOOBY-DOO!"

GLOSSARY

cargo objects carried by a ship, aircraft or other vehicle

galley kitchen on a ship

landlubber someone who is not used to living or working at sea

legendary well known

meddling interfering with someone else's business

pesky annoying

plank long board that goes off the side of a ship; similar to a diving board

tycoon business person who is rich and powerful

AUTHOR

John Sazaklis is a *New York Times* best-selling author with almost 100 children's books under his utility belt! He has also illustrated Spider-Man books, created toys for *MAD* magazine, and written for the BEN 10 animated series. John lives in New York, USA, with his superpowered wife and daughter.

ILLUSTRATOR

Christian Cornia is a character designer, illustrator and comic artist from Modena, Italy. He has created artwork for publishers, advertisers and video games. He currently teaches character design at the Scuola Internazionale di Comics of Reggio Emilia. Christian works digitally but remains a secret lover of the pencil, and he doesn't go anywhere without a sketchbook in his bag.

TALK ABOUT IT

1. The Mystery Inc. gang is often chasing ghosts. Do you believe in ghosts? Why or why not?

2. Do you think it was a good idea for the team to split up? What would you have done?

3. What would have happened if the team hadn't caught the pirate ghost?

WRITE ABOUT IT

1. Make a list of people you would want on your mystery-solving team. Next to each name, add a reason why you want that person on your team.

2. Would you rather be part of a team or solve a mystery on your own? Write a few sentences about your decision.

3. Write a short story featuring your favourite members of the Mystery Inc. team. Put them in an adventure or describe them solving a mystery!

Help solve mystery after mystery with Scooby-Doo and the gang!

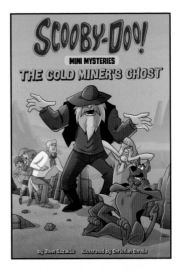

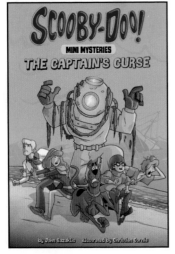

NEW TITLES!